I Miss My Best Friend

By Penelope Lagos

Illustrated by Sophie Moracchini

GreenTree Publishers
Newnan, Georgia

I Miss My Best Friend
Copyright © 2017 by Penelope Lagos

Printed in the United States of America
ISBN-13: 978-1-944483-14-2 (GreenTree Publishers)
ISBN-10: 1-944483-14-4

GreenTree Publishers
www.greentreepublishers.com

In Loving Memory of my best friend,
Cassius "The Legend" Lagos.
To all of those who have loved and lost,
this story is about my family,
but it is written for you.

Louie and Penny were twins who loved animals. When they were little, they begged their parents for a dog almost every day.

"When you're old enough to help take care of a dog, we'll get one," Mom promised.

When the twins turned six-years-old, their parents took them to the animal shelter. Louie and Penny immediately fell in love with a puppy. His fur was as white as snow.

Louie pointed to a brown patch over the puppy's left eye. "That reminds me of a pirate!" he laughed.

"That's the one," Penny exclaimed. Louie agreed.

The puppy seemed to understand. His little tail wagged as he lifted his paw up high.

"We should name him Cassius," Louie said.

"That's a great name," Penny shouted. "It sounds strong."

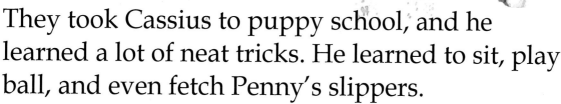

They took Cassius to puppy school, and he learned a lot of neat tricks. He learned to sit, play ball, and even fetch Penny's slippers.

Cassius became part of the family. When they went on vacation, he went with them.

When Penny and Louie came home from school, he greeted them. When they had a bad day, Cassius always put smiles on their faces.

"You're our best friend," Penny said as she hugged their dog.

Louie joined her. "We love you, Cassius."

11

They went on hikes and played in the park
for hours.

Cassius even became a champion swimmer.

At the end of each day, he was ready for bed. He took turns sleeping with Louie and Penny.

Everyone in town knew and loved him. The veterinarian's office even nick-named him "Good Boy" because he was their best patient. Even the neighborhood cat made friends with him.

Cassius grew older. When he turned ten-years-old, the twins could tell going on trips and playing ball made him very tired.

Cassius had always been a happy dog. Now, he seemed sad.

Mom knelt down and put her hand on his head. "I think you might be sick, Cassius."

"We should take him to the vet," Penny said.

Louie packed Cassius' favorite blanket. The ride to the office was a lot longer and quieter than normal.

In the past, Penny enjoyed taking Cassius to the vet. Today was different. She felt sad and worried about their dog.

When a girl walked in with a puppy, Cassius didn't even raise his head. Normally, he would have been eager to greet another animal.

Louie leaned over and hugged Cassius. "You don't feel well, do you, buddy?"

25

The vet had bad news for them. Cassius was not going to get better. He was very sick.

It was time to say goodbye to their best friend. They each took turns hugging and kissing him one last time.

"We love you, Cassius," Penny said.

At home, Penny and Louie cried and cried. Nothing seemed to make them feel better. They missed their best friend.

"Get a new puppy," friends suggested. No one seemed to understand that Cassius was much more than just a pet to the twins.

Louie and Penny told their stories and shared their memories about Cassius. They created a beautiful memorial in the backyard for him. They made a scrapbook of photos and kept journals to write down their feelings. They even volunteered at the animal shelter where they first met Cassius.

One day, while Penny and Louie were helping out at the animal shelter, a little boy and girl came in looking for their first puppy. It reminded the twins of their search for a little buddy years earlier.

The little boy turned to his sister and said, "Sis, which one is your favorite? I want the one with the black patch."

Penny remembered this excitement well. She picked up the little pup and handed it to the girl.

"He will be your best friend forever," Penny told the excited children. She looked at Louie and smiled, "I miss *my* best friend."

Louie hugged her tight and said, "Sis, true friendships never die."

Tips to Cope with Pet Loss

1. Give your child permission to grieve and speak freely and honestly about their pet. Be open to questions.

2. Reassurance is key. Provide lots of hugs and emotional support.

3. Create a memorial, photo collage/scrapbook as a tribute.

4. Let your child express his/her feelings through art or writing.

5. Make your child's teacher aware of the loss.

6. Plant a special tree or flower to honor your pet.

7. Invite family and friends over to share their happy memories.

8. Post a photo and memorial on a pet bereavement site.

9. Donate/Volunteer at your local shelter in memory of your pet.

10. Maintain a normal routine.

About the Author

Penelope Lagos, a New Jersey native, graduated from Rutgers University earning a BA in Communications and Theatre Arts. She is a huge animal advocate and strongly believes in being "a voice for the voiceless." She holds a certification in Canine Fitness and Conditioning as well as Advanced Pet CPR/First Aid. Her love of animals, and loss of her beloved best friend Cassius "The Legend" Lagos, inspired her to write "I Miss My Best Friend" and help others cope with the grief of losing a family pet. When Penelope is not spending time with her own furry friends, you will find her acting in indie films and commercials as well as volunteering at The Leukemia and Lymphoma Society. Penelope was the recipient of an achievement award honoring critical funds raised for LLS.

You can contact Penelope through her website at www.penelopelagos.com.

Cassius "The Legend" Lagos
12/30/99 - 7/17/15

Made in the USA
Lexington, KY
01 October 2017